ID0407295

Other Books by Gery Greer and Bob Ruddick

Chapter Books

Let Me Off This Spaceship!

Jason and the Aliens Down the Street
American Bookseller "Pick of the Lists" 1991

Jason and the Lizard Pirates

Middle Grade Books

Max and Me and the Time Machine
American Bookseller "Pick of the Lists" 1983
School Library Journal Best Books of 1983
CBS *Storybreak* animated television episode (first
    airing in 1987)

This Island Isn't Big Enough for the Four of Us!
South Dakota Prairie Pasque Children's Book
    Award Winner 1990
Utah Children's Literature Award Winner 1990
Minnesota Lovelace Book Award Winner 1992

NOV 0 0 1994

JASON
and the
ESCAPE
from
BAT PLANET

by GERY GREER and BOB RUDDICK
Illustrations by
BLANCHE L. SIMS

HarperCollins*Publishers*

For Larissa

Jason and the Escape from Bat Planet
Text copyright © 1993 by Gery Greer and Bob Ruddick
Illustrations copyright © 1993 by Blanche L. Sims
All rights reserved. No part of this book may be used or reproduced in any manner whatsoever without written permission except in the case of brief quotations embodied in critical articles and reviews. Printed in the United States of America. For information address HarperCollins Children's Books, a division of HarperCollins Publishers, 10 East 53rd Street, New York, NY 10022.

Typography by Tom Starace
1 2 3 4 5 6 7 8 9 10
❖
First Edition

Library of Congress Cataloging-in-Publication Data
Greer, Gery.
  Jason and the escape from Bat Planet / by Gery Greer and Bob Ruddick ; illustrations by Blanche L. Sims.
      p.   cm.
  Summary: Jason, Cooper Vor, and Lootna grapple with General Batso and his evil Demon Bats in the further adventures of the Intragalactic Troubleshooting Team.
  ISBN 0-06-021221-7. — ISBN 0-06-021222-5 (lib. bdg.)
  [1. Science Fiction.   2. Extraterrestrial beings—Fiction.]   I. Ruddick, Bob.   II. Sims, Blanche, ill.   III. Title.
PZ7.G85347Jase   1993   92-41169
[Fic]—dc20   CIP
                                                                AC

"**F**IVE BUCKS," SAID Arnold. "Give me five bucks, Jason, and this fantastic hat is yours. Five measly bucks. What do you say?"

Arnold Crump was waving a bright-yellow hat under my nose. It was shaped like a duck. A big, smiling, silly-looking duck with webbed feet that flopped down on either side, over your ears. He had won it at an amusement park.

"Forget it, Arnold," I said. "I'm not buying the hat. It's a dumb hat, and I wouldn't wear it if it was the last hat on Earth."

"Okay, then, four bucks," said Arnold. "Four measly bucks. You're dying to have this hat, Jason. I can see it in your eyes."

I sighed. I should have known better than to go to a garage sale at Arnold's house. I mean, he's not the sort of person who will let you poke around in peace. He's more the sort of person who will drive you *stark raving crazy*.

The fact is, Arnold is very big on money. And he's always thinking up ways to make more of it. Gobs and gobs of it. He's probably got more gobs in the bank than most grown-ups do. Today he was having the "Garage Sale of the Century."

I shook my head firmly. "Read my lips, Arnold," I said. "You've got the wrong guy. I do not wear animals on my head."

Arnold held the hat out at arm's length and looked at it in an admiring way. "This is no ordinary duck hat, Jason. This is a genuine Mr. Duckles the Duck hat. It glows in the dark."

"I don't care if it *quacks* in the dark," I said. "I'm still not interested."

"Three bucks," said Arnold. "We're talking cheap here, Jason."

"We're talking *no* here, Arnold. Forget it. You're quacking up the wrong tree."

"One buck? I think Mr. Duckles likes you."

"Give up, Arnold."

"But—"

Suddenly my watch began to bleep. *Bleep! Bleep! Bleep!*

I gulped. Then I whipped my hand

behind my back. Not here! I thought. Not now! Why can't this thing go off when there's no one else around?

You see, my watch may look like a regular watch, but it's not. It's very special and very secret. It's called a communicator watch, and you can't buy one like it anywhere in America. In fact, you can't buy one like it anywhere on Earth.

The truth is, an alien from outer space gave it to me.

"You know what, Arnold?" I said. "I think I'll take a look in those boxes over there."

Before he could say anything, I hurried over to the other side of the garage. I knelt down beside a big box full of old toys. Then I cupped my hand around my communicator watch and peered down at it.

The watch face had faded away. It had become a tiny TV screen.

And there on the screen was the tanned, smiling face of Cooper Vor—the very same alien from outer space who had given me the watch.

"Hi, Jason!" said Coop. "Don't you just love these communicator watches? Listen, I've got a question for you."

Coop lives four houses down the street from me. He looks like an ordinary human, but actually he's from a planet on the far side of the galaxy. Not long ago he hired me to be his assistant. Now we go on missions to outer space together.

Coop's an Intragalactic Troubleshooter. That means that anybody in the galaxy can hire him to solve any kind of problem. And I don't mean *small* problems. Somehow they always seem to be *big* problems—of the very, very risky variety. I think Coop likes it that way.

"Hi, Coop," I whispered into my watch. I glanced over my shoulder at Arnold. He was busy with another customer. "Sure, go ahead. Ask away."

"How do you feel about Demon Bats?" he asked.

"Uh, Demon Bats?" I whispered. "What are Demon Bats?"

"Big batlike creatures," said Coop. "About your size. Thousands of them, living on the planet Bluggax. They've thrown a friend of mine in jail, so we have a rescue mission on our hands. We've got to break him out before it's too late."

"A jailbreak?" I said. My voice came out kind of squeaky.

"Right," said Coop. He chuckled. "I figure we can have a little fun with this one. There shouldn't be any problems—unless the Demon Bats catch us sneaking around, of course. They're related to the vampire bat, and they do like a sip of blood now and then. How soon can you get over here?"

I swallowed hard. "Uh, let's see . . . five minutes?"

"Good," said Coop. "Over and out."

"Over and out."

I stood up and started out of the garage. But Arnold blocked my way. He was holding something tall and black in his hand.

"Perhaps I can interest you in this beautiful work of art," he said. "It's a magnificent hand-carved statue of an eagle.

The eagle is the most noble of all birds, you know. It's the symbol of our nation. Ten bucks, Jason. A mere ten bucks and this beauty is yours forever."

"That's not an eagle," I pointed out. "It's a buzzard."

Arnold looked shocked. "Buzzard? Did you say buzzard? Surely you're mistaken. How does five bucks sound to you?"

I sighed. "I'll take the duck hat," I said.

"Huh?"

"I'll take the duck hat."

I figured the fastest way to get out of there was to buy something. And the hat was the cheapest thing I'd seen.

I handed Arnold a dollar, which made him pretty happy. He handed me the duck hat. I wadded it up and stuffed it in my pocket. Then I hurried out of the garage.

"Hey, Jason!" Arnold called after me.

I looked back over my shoulder.

"Don't forget that your hat is guaranteed," he called. "If it isn't all it's quacked up to be, just bring it back for a full refund." Then he whooped with laughter. "Get it? *Quacked* up to be?"

I chuckled as I hopped on my bike. Sometimes Arnold was all right.

"Ho, ho," I called back. "That really quacks me up!"

CHAPTER 2

"**T**HIS MESSAGE CAME in half an hour ago," said Coop. "What do you make of it?"

I was sitting in Cooper Vor's den, which looks pretty much like anyone else's den. Except that the sofa opens up into a huge computer. It was open now, since that's how the message had arrived.

Coop handed me the printout and I read it.

COOP—
HAVE MADE UNFORTUNATE MIS-
TAKE. HAVE TURNED GENERAL
BATSO OF BLUGGAX BRIGHT
PINK. MISTAKES WILL HAPPEN,
BUT GENERAL BATSO NOT
AMUSED. PROMISES TO TOSS
ME OFF CLIFF AT SUNSET.
MEANWHILE, HAVE BEEN
THROWN INTO JAIL. REQUEST
IMMEDIATE RESCUE. FIND
MILE-HIGH CLIFF. ENTER LEFT
NOSTRIL. PROCEED 100 PACES
STRAIGHT AHEAD, THEN 100
PACES STRAIGHT UP. HOPE TO
SEE YOU SOON. THE SOONER
THE BETTER!
            YOUR FRIEND,
            F. I.

I looked at Coop.

"Enter left nostril?" I said. "We're supposed to enter somebody's *nose*? Or is this some kind of code?"

"You got me," said Coop cheerfully. "I'm as puzzled as you are. But don't worry. I'm sure we'll be able to figure it out once we get to Bluggax."

I glanced at the message again. "Who's General Batso?" I asked.

"He's the leader of the Demon Bats and a very tough customer," said Coop. "Beady red eyes, needle-sharp fangs, big black leathery wings. Let's just say he's not the sort of bat you'd want to meet in a dark alley."

Or even a nice, bright, sunny alley, I thought.

"Also," Coop went on, "he's very proud

of his looks. He comes in first in the Mr. Muscle competition on Bluggax each year, and he never lets anyone forget it."

"And now your friend has turned him pink?" I asked. "Boy, no wonder this General Batso is mad. How'd it happen?"

Coop shrugged. "Beats me. Must have been an accident of some kind. I mean, Finny Ikkit is brilliant, but—"

"Finny Ikkit?" I broke in excitedly. I'd heard that name before. "You mean the same Finny Ikkit who invented the secret weapon we used on our last mission? That's your friend? That's who sent the message?"

Coop nodded. "None other," he said. "Believe me, Jason, the man's a genius! The man's brilliant! Search the galaxy and you won't find a more talented inventor. You name it, Finny Ikkit can invent it."

"*Ha!*" came a voice from the doorway. "Who are you kidding? That idiot Finny Ikkit couldn't invent his way out of a wet paper bag!"

CHAPTER 3

I SPUN AROUND.

It was Lootna, the third member of our troubleshooting team. She padded into the den on her four paws, holding some sort of map with her tail.

Lootna is a beautiful black cat creature. True, she looks a little like a rabbit because of her long ears. And a little like a monkey because of her long tail. But mostly she looks like a very large cat with silky black fur and glowing purple eyes. She's from the planet Ganx.

"Hi, Jason," she said. "I suppose Cooper's told you the news. The biggest numbskull in the galaxy has gotten himself in a pickle. And now *we* have to risk our necks to get him out!"

She looked pretty disgusted as she jumped up on a table and sat down.

"Now, Lootna . . ." Coop began.

Lootna's purple eyes flashed. "The very same numbskull, I might add, whose crazy invention almost got us eaten by Lizard Pirates on our last mission. Brilliant inventor, my foot! The man's a menace."

"Now, Lootna," said Coop with a grin. "We got out alive, didn't we? Besides, you have to admit that Finny's invention was pretty amazing. It just wasn't what we were expecting, that's all."

19

"Hmmpf," sniffed Lootna. "It certainly wasn't. In fact, the only good thing about *this* mission is that I'll have a chance to give that Finny Ikkit a piece of my mind."

Her long black tail began to swish back and forth. And that's when she noticed that she was still holding something with it.

"Oh, I almost forgot," she said. "I searched the Sector T-32 files and found that map of Bluggax you asked for, Cooper."

"Good work," said Coop. He took the map and quickly scanned it. "Aha! Here's the Mile-High Cliff. We'll begin our search for the mystery nostril there."

Coop folded the map and tucked it in his pocket. "Now we'd better make tracks," he said. Turning toward the door, he suddenly shouted, *"Race you to the spaceship!"*

And he went running out of the den.

Lootna and I exchanged a startled glance. Then we jumped up and ran after him.

"Oh, great," Lootna said as we went tearing through the living room. "When was the last time you heard of a captain racing his crew to the spaceship? Will this man *ever* grow up?"

But I noticed that Lootna was taking the race pretty seriously herself. She put on a burst of speed as we galloped down the hallway. And when Coop paused to open the door to the garage, she went streaking past him.

"I won!" she said as she bounded up onto the hood of the spaceship.

Coop and I jogged into the garage after her. "I've never beaten Lootna in a footrace yet," he told me with a grin. "But there's always a first time."

"Dream on," said Lootna. She began smugly washing her paws.

The garage is where Coop keeps his spaceship—a long, sleek two-man flyer with swept-back wings on the sides and a bubble top over the cockpit. Actually, it's kind of hard even to see it. The spaceship is painted with a special camouflage paint called Startint so that it changes color to blend in with its surroundings.

Coop pressed a button on his watch. I knew what was going to happen, but I was still amazed. The whole back wall suddenly disappeared. Just like that. No more wall.

In place of the wall—from floor to ceiling and from one side to the other—all you could see was blue. Just a huge, strange, beautiful square of deep, deep blue.

It was Coop's wormhole into space. By flying through there, we could pop out almost anywhere in the galaxy. All it takes is a couple of seconds—and a little know-how, of course.

Coop opened the bubble top and jumped into the spaceship. "All aboard for the planet of the Demon Bats!" he said.

A small shiver went up my spine as I hurried around to the other side and climbed in next to him.

Who cares if these Demon Bats have fangs? I tried to tell myself. Fangs are just teeth, aren't they? Big deal. They have to brush them just like the rest of us do, don't they?

Lootna twitched her tail a couple of times. Then she made a flying leap over the two of us and landed in the space behind our seats.

Coop closed the bubble top and fired up the engine. A high-pitched whine filled the air, and I could feel the spaceship vibrating on its launch tracks. Ahead was the nothingness of the blue wormhole.

"Are we ready?" asked Coop.

Lootna snorted. "Who's ever ready to face a planet full of thousands of bloodthirsty, beady-eyed Demon Bats?"

Coop grinned. "Hey, we Intragalactic Troubleshooters welcome a little danger. It sharpens our wits and keeps us on our toes. Right, Jason?"

"Right," I said. Then I looked around to see if it was really me who had said it.

"Blast off!" said Coop, pushing a lever forward. The spaceship hurtled straight ahead into the square of blue.

I hardly had time to blink before we burst out another wormhole. The spaceship did a half roll. Then it dived.

And then it leveled off above a bright-yellow sea. Huge waves tossed beneath us.

There was no land in sight.

CHAPTER 4

COOP CHECKED THE map. "Three minutes to the Mile-High Cliff," he said. "Keep your eyes peeled. And if anybody sees a nostril, sing out."

We were zooming along at high speed, barely clearing the tops of the yellow waves. I glanced up through the bubble top. Fluffy white clouds were floating in a pale-green sky.

"A *nostril?*" muttered Lootna. "Why can't that Finny Ikkit write a message that makes sense? *What* nostril? *Whose*

26

thought. Did he mean "jump" out of the spaceship"?

ble top popped open. And as
ip slid slowly by the dark
ed out one at a time. When it
, I pushed off hard, making
ok down.

last. He was carrying a back-
d grabbed from behind his
er had his feet hit the rock
spaceship picked up speed.
toward the clouds and out

o there we were. On our
ile above the yellow sea,
ng, round, dark tunnel.
some sort of air vent,"
p. "These nostril tunnels

nostril? If you ask me, this Ikkit fellow isn't hitting on all cylinders."

Just then we spotted a low rim of land on the horizon. "That must be our cliff," said Coop.

He changed our heading slightly, and we sped toward the rim. As we did, a fantastic cliff seemed to rise slowly up from the sea. Higher . . . higher . . .

I'd never seen anything like it. Far to the left and right it stretched—a wall of rock a mile high, plunging straight into the water. Enormous waves crashed against the base.

Suddenly I saw something else. Coop and Lootna saw it, too.

"Nostrils!" we all shouted together.

Actually, what we saw was a whole face. Dead ahead and halfway up the cliff was a gigantic face carved into the rock. It had large pointed ears, glaring eyes, an ugly snout, and a gaping mouth with sharp fangs.

A bat face.

"Spooky," I said. "Look at the size of that mouth."

"It's big, all right," said Coop. "Must be the main entrance to the Demon Bats' cave city. That cliff is probably riddled with caverns and tunnels and teeming with bats. But we're in luck. There's no one in sight. Maybe we can make it to the left nostril without being seen."

We were still racing toward the base of the cliff, hugging the waves. We were closing in fast. Too fast!

But at the last moment Coop pulled the nose of the spaceship up sharply. And

probably bring fresh air into the cave system. Let's see where this one leads."

We sneaked slowly in. Finny's message had said to go a hundred paces straight ahead and then a hundred paces straight up. Coop counted off each step as we went.

At fifty paces it was too dark to see. Coop switched on a small light on his communicator watch. I did the same.

". . . ninety-eight . . . ninety-nine . . . one hundred."

We stopped and looked up. Directly above us was a vertical air shaft. It was just as large and round and black as the tunnel we were in.

But there was no ladder in sight. And no footholds. There was no way up.

"Well?" whispered Lootna. "I give up. How are we going to go a hundred paces straight up? Or did someone happen to bring along a trampoline in his back pocket? Or a hot-air balloon, maybe?"

"Say no more," said Coop. "I came prepared."

He took off his backpack and dumped a bunch of weird-looking metal things out onto the tunnel floor. They had straps on one side and lots of little suction cups on the other.

"Sucker feet!" he announced in high spirits. "Brand new, high-tech sucker feet. All we have to do is slip these babies onto our hands and feet, and we can walk up walls just as pretty as you please."

"Wow, great!" I said.

"They've got everything," Coop went on. "Automatic balancers, high-performance silencers, power push, the works. I've been waiting for a good excuse to try them out, and this is it. We'll climb up to Finny's jail cell, cut through the bars, and climb back down again as easy as one, two, three. So buckle up and let's move out."

"Hold it, hold it, hold it!" said Lootna. "Not so fast, Cooper Vor. Before I risk my life climbing up some dark, drafty hole in the rock, I've got one teeny-weeny little question. Just exactly who invented these sucker-feet thingamajigs?"

"Why, Finny Ikkit, of course," said Coop with a grin. "That's the beauty of it. We're going to use one of Finny's own inventions to rescue him. Neat, huh?"

Lootna clapped her paw to her forehead and groaned. Then she turned to me and said, "Our sucker feet were invented by the biggest squidbrain in the galaxy. Get ready to go *splat*."

BUT TEN MINUTES later we were high up the air shaft. And nobody had gone *splat* yet.

Clinging to the wall, I removed a hand and placed it higher. . . . Now a foot . . .

I don't know how Finny Ikkit did it, but his sucker feet made walking up walls a breeze. And there wasn't a sound as we moved slowly upward. The silencers were working perfectly.

"Well!" whispered Lootna happily. "I must admit we do seem to be going up!"

Lootna was climbing next to me. She

had small sucker feet attached to all four paws. "Yes, perhaps I was a bit too hard on Mr. Ikkit," she went on. "Perhaps he doesn't have a poached egg for a brain after all. This is actually quite delightful, isn't it? How high are we, Cooper?"

"Forty-two paces and counting," said Coop in a low voice. "Hey, look. There's a light up ahead."

I pushed away from the wall so I could get a better look. Some distance above us a dim, greenish light was coming through an opening in the wall of the air shaft.

"But that can't be Finny's jail cell," I whispered. "We aren't high enough yet."

Coop nodded. "It's something else," he agreed. "But what?"

As quietly as three flies on a wall, we crept up to the opening. It was a large square hole covered with wire mesh. We peered through . . .

Into a cavern. An enormous cavern. And we were looking into it from a point high up near its ceiling.

Something weird was happening.

Flap, flap, flap, flap, flap, flap!

A stream of big black Demon Bats was flying into the cavern through a large round doorway in the opposite wall. In single file they wheeled up in a wide arc, then swooped back down to the cavern floor. They landed at attention, snapping their huge black wings shut.

There they stood, side by side in long rows. Eyes front, shoulders back.

In front of them, facing them, stood one bat.

He was broad-shouldered, barrel-

chested, and about my height. He stood with his short legs wide apart and his clenched fists on his hips. A fierce scowl was on his bat face. His wings kept slowly unfolding and folding, unfolding and folding—like a huge leathery fan.

No doubt about it. This was one angry bat.

And this was one *pink* bat. Wings, ears, face, feet—everything was bright pink.

"It's General Batso," whispered Coop. "A bit pink, isn't he?"

"You can say that again," whispered Lootna. "No wonder your friend Finny Ikkit got tossed in jail."

The last of the bats landed neatly at attention at the end of the back row. Now there was total silence in the cavern.

Finally Batso spoke. "All right, *who did it?*" he thundered. "Who wrote the poem?"

He paused. There wasn't a sound.

"Somebody in this room stuck this poem on one of our walls!" boomed General Batso. He waved a piece of paper in the air. "I found it myself not fifteen minutes ago."

He held the paper out in front of him and read it aloud:

He's pink! He's pink!
So pink he makes you blink!
His nose is pink!
His toes are pink!
A big fat bat who's pink!

General Batso slowly folded his arms

across his muscular chest. He narrowed his beady red eyes. There was a lot of nervous shuffling of feet among the troops.

"All right, so we've got a funnyman among us, do we?" thundered the general. "A regular comedian, eh? Well, I've got news for everyone, so listen up! *Nobody* is leaving this cave until the bat who wrote that poem steps forward and admits it!"

Nobody moved.

"Fine!" snapped General Batso. "Fine and dandy! Then we'll all just stand right here until someone confesses. I've got all the time in the world."

He glared at his troops. "And get this and get it good," he added. "I am *not* pink! Doesn't anyone around here know anything about colors? I'm just very slightly pinkish, that's all. That idiot Finny Ikkit just turned me very slightly pinkish!"

Just then Coop nudged Lootna and me and gave an upward jerk of his head.

"Speaking of Finny," he whispered, "we'd better sneak on up and bust him out of jail while our bat friends are busy."

We started climbing again.

Sixty paces . . . seventy . . . eighty . . . KA-THWOP! . . . KA-THWOP!

What the . . . ? I thought.

The silencer on one of Lootna's sucker feet had fallen off!

And now another! And another!

Good grief. Now three of her sucker feet made loud sucking sounds whenever she pulled them off the wall. She sounded like a bull elephant trying to walk through thick glue.

KA-THWOP! . . . KA-THWOP! . . . KA-THWOP! The sound echoed up and down the air shaft.

Almost immediately *another* sound echoed up and down the air shaft.

The sound of General Batso's voice.

"SOMEBODY'S IN THE AIR SHAFT!"

"**Q**UICK!" SAID COOP. "We'll hide out in Finny's jail cell till we figure out our next move."

The three of us scrambled higher. I've never moved faster in my life.

KA-THWOP! . . . KA-THWOP! . . . KA-THWOP!

"Just wait'll I get my paws on that nitwit inventor," growled Lootna. "Si-lencers! *Ha!* I've heard more silence in the middle of a giant Destructo Tornado on the storm planet of Naxos."

We reached Finny Ikkit's jail cell. In the wall of the air shaft was a window with iron bars. Behind the bars was a fat little man with big cuplike ears and wild green hair. He was wearing some sort of weird jumpsuit covered with pockets. His green eyes were twinkling with delight.

"Cooper Vor!" he cried. "I knew you'd come! And I see you're using my very own sucker feet. Good choice, good choice! They're a rather nifty invention, if I do say so myself."

"You . . . you . . . you . . ." sputtered Lootna.

"Hi, Finny," said Coop. "How's it going?"

"Let me at him!" said Lootna.

Coop and I switched on the lasers on our communicator watches. Then we

used them to cut through the bars as if they were butter. We pushed the bars into the room, and the three of us tumbled in after them.

No sooner had we slipped off our sucker feet than Lootna marched over and stabbed her paw at the little round man.

"So *you're* Mr. Finny Ikkit!" she burst out. "I have a thing or two I'd like to discuss with *you*, bub. Of all the stupid—"

"Why, you must be Miss Lootna of Ganx," Finny broke in. He gave a sweeping bow and then turned to Coop. "Shame on you, Cooper," he said, waggling his finger at him. "You never told me what a beautiful, charming creature she is!"

That caught Lootna off guard. Her jaw dropped open and she stared at Finny.

And before she could get her mouth going again, Finny had turned to me.

"And you must be Jason Harkness, the Earth boy," he said, pumping my hand. "Coop's told me all about you. So good of you to come to my rescue. I'm afraid General Batso is rather angry with me. It's this 'pink' business, you know."

"Yes, I know," I said politely. "Uh, how'd it happen?"

"Yeah, how?" asked Lootna. Then she added under her breath, "Not that I'm surprised, of course."

"Well, it all started," said Finny, "when General Batso asked me to invent a machine that would allow him to walk through walls."

"Through *walls*?" asked Coop, looking interested.

48

"Exactly," said Finny. "Batso told me he was going to a surprise party for a friend, and he wanted to be able to step right through the wall and yell, 'Surprise! Surprise!' Well, that sounded like a very nice idea to me. You know how much I love a good party, Cooper. So I invented the machine."

"Brilliant!" said Coop. "So with your machine, General Batso could actually walk through walls?"

"No, it turned him pink instead," said Finny.

"Of course," muttered Lootna. "What else?"

"There was a slight problem with the molecular separator ray, I believe," said Finny. "But never mind, it served Batso right. I found out later he wasn't going to a surprise party at all. He only wanted to walk through walls so he could rob the Great Gold Vault on Vargas, the scoundrel."

"Doesn't surprise me a bit, Finny," said Coop. "That Batso's a bad egg. But bats will be bats, you know. I once knew a bat who . . . Wait. What's that noise?"

We listened.

And heard the distant sound of flapping wings coming from the other side of the cell door. Bat wings, and lots of them. Closer and closer they came—flapping, whapping, snapping. It sounded like the entire army of Demon Bats was on the move.

The flapping stopped on the other side of Finny's jail cell door. We froze, hardly breathing.

Then we heard that voice again. General Batso's voice.

"Jailer, open this door! The intruders could be inside!"

CHAPTER 7

THERE WAS A SHORT silence. Then we heard a different bat voice say, "We've got a problem, sir."

"Well, what is it, jailer?" snapped General Batso.

"I forgot the key, sir."

"You *what*?"

"It was all the excitement, sir. I left it with my key chain, sir."

"Well, where's your key chain, you knucklehead?"

"It's on my belt, sir."

"Well, blast it! *Where's your belt?*"

"In my office, sir. It's gotten a bit too tight for me to buckle up properly. All those jellypuffs, you know."

"No, I do *not* know. And I do not *want* to know. Now you flap yourself back to that office and get that key, or I'll tie your wings together and toss you off the cliff!"

"Yes, sir. You bet, sir. I'm out of here, sir. By the way, would you like me to bring you a jell—"

"NO! You bring me a jellypuff and you're history, mister! Just *bring me that key!*"

"On the double, sir."

We heard the sound of bat wings flapping rapidly down the hall. Coop gave a signal and the four of us quickly formed a huddle.

"Okay, gang," whispered Coop. "As I see it, we've got two problems. First, those bats will be coming through that door any minute. And second, we can't go back out the air shaft, because they've probably got it guarded at both ends. In other words, we're trapped. But never fear. An Intragalactic Troubleshooter always has a backup plan. So I have *this*."

He whipped an odd-shaped gray box out of his pocket. It was covered with tiny pinholes and had a red button on top.

"Hey, that's one of my Tiny-izers!" said Finny happily. "A little invention I whipped up just for the fun of it."

"Well, it's about to save our lives," said Coop. "All we have to do is stand close to this box, push that button, and *poof*. It makes us tiny."

"Amazing!" I whispered. "How tiny?"

"About the size of a pea," said Finny. "Give or take a smidgen. And the Tiny-izer turns itself tiny, too."

"After we're small," explained Coop, "we can hide behind that table leg over there. Those bats will never find us." He chuckled at the beauty of it all. "And when they leave, we can just sneak under the door and hoof it for home."

"Hey, not so fast," hissed Lootna. "How do I know this Tiny-izer gadget really works? How do I know it isn't going to turn me into a frog? Or maybe a wart? A *tiny* wart. And how do I know—"

There was a loud pounding of fists on the jail door. "Are the intruders in there with you, Finny?" roared General Batso. "If they are, I'll suck their veins dry!"

"On second thought," whispered Lootna, "what are we waiting for? Let's get tiny!"

Coop quickly pushed the red button on the box.

Za-a-ap! Za-a-ap! Little white lightning bolts shot out of the box in all directions, zapping right through our bodies.

And the next thing I knew—POW!—I was *huge*! I must have been twelve feet tall! And Coop, Lootna, and Finny were giants, too. We were so enormous we filled the entire room—doubled over in a jumble of elbows, knees, hands, and feet. We couldn't move.

"Well!" said Finny from somewhere under my arm. "Now that was a surprise, wasn't it?"

I looked down. Lootna's face was

pressed up near Finny's face. "This is *tiny*?" she sputtered. "This is the size of a *pea*? I'll tell you what's the size of a pea, Finny Ikkit. Your brain!"

"You know, your eyes really are an amazing color of purple when they flash that way," observed Finny.

Flap, flap, flap! Bat wings, approaching fast. The jailer was returning with the key!

"Quick," whispered Coop. "We've got to push that button again. Where's the Tiny-izer?"

"Beats me," whispered Finny. "We're so squashed together I can't even wiggle my ears, let alone move my head."

"I see it," I whispered. "It's bigger now, but I can't reach it. It's on the floor between Coop's knee and Lootna's hip.

Lootna, can you move your tail?"

She wiggled it. "A little," she grumped. "No thanks to Mr. Ikkit."

"Okay," I said. "Maybe you can use the tip of your tail to push the button. Try moving it to the left. Forward a little . . . Now down, down . . . Okay, good. Push."

Lootna pressed down on the button with her tail.

Za-a-ap! Za-a-ap! POW! It worked! We were our normal sizes again.

Just then we heard General Batso's voice booming from the other side of the door. "All right, jailer, what took you so long? And what's that on the side of your mouth? It had better not be jellypuff!"

"No, sir. Absolutely not, sir. That's from yesterday, sir. That's—"

"Never mind! Just give me the key!"

Coop grabbed Finny by the shoulders. "Quick, Finny. Your walk-through-walls invention. The one that turned Batso pink. Do you think it might work properly this time?"

Finny fished something small and shiny out of one of his many pockets. It looked sort of like a flashlight with three tiny legs. "Well, I've tinkered with it a bit," he said. "But I can't guarantee it'll work. It might just turn us pink instead."

"That's a chance we'll have to take," said Coop.

Lootna groaned. "I knew it was going to be one of those days," she said.

We heard the sound of a key rattling in the lock.

Finny quickly set the machine down on a small table so that it was aiming at us and flicked a switch. A wide beam of sparkling pink light came streaming out of the machine, flooding over us. My skin prickled.

I glanced down at my hand. At least I wasn't turning pink.

The door burst open! Demon Bats poured into the room. Their red eyes gleamed, and their clawlike hands stretched out for us. General Batso led the charge.

"Gotcha!" he cried.

"Wanna bet?" yelled Coop.

The four of us raced toward the side wall. Coop snatched the walk-through-walls machine off the table as we passed.

I felt a claw grabbing at my shoulder as I met the wall, face first.

But then suddenly we were on the other side!

Just the four of us.

In an empty room.

CHAPTER 8

*W*HAM! SLAM! *"OOF!"*

"Ouch!" We could hear the sound of bats crashing into the wall behind us.

And then General Batso's angry voice: "What? They went through the wall! Quick! Circle around and cut them off!"

Coop checked the direction finder on his communicator watch.

"This way!" he said, pointing. "With a little luck we can make it to the spaceship."

We dashed across the room and

through the wall on the far side. Into another empty room. Then another. I couldn't feel a thing as we passed through the walls. It was as if they weren't even there.

"Terrific invention, Finny," I said over my shoulder.

"I do my best," said Finny modestly.

"I think the tips of my ears have turned pink," said Lootna.

We cut across a huge corridor lit with pale-green light. I glanced at the wall as we passed through it. The light was coming from thousands of tiny green glow-worms.

Now we were racing through a storage room filled with strange, spearlike weapons. They were hanging from stalactites or propped up against stalagmites.

"Do my ears look pink to you?" Lootna asked me. She wiggled them in front of me as we ran.

"No, they look fine, Lootna," I said.

Suddenly we burst through a wall into a pitch-black room, so dark that we couldn't see the tips of our noses. We stopped and stood frozen, letting our eyes adjust to the darkness.

I gave a shiver. Wherever we were, it was cold and musty and silent. Something about this place felt wrong. The hair on the back of my neck rose.

Then I realized something. The cave *wasn't* silent. A faint sound seemed to be coming from everywhere around us. I strained to hear. It was a strange sucking and sighing sound, like wind gusting under a door.

All of a sudden I knew . . . and my heart almost stopped. Breathing! It was the sound of breathing!

Now I could make out dim shapes in the darkness. But what I saw didn't make me feel any better. We were in a long, low cavern with thin rods stretching from wall to wall, near the ceiling. From the rods hung dozens of huge black shapes in long rows, like giant slabs of beef.

It took me a second to realize they were Demon Bats. Hanging upside down with their heads a few inches off the floor. Sleeping. We had stumbled into a dormitory.

Coop put his finger to his lips to signal silence. Then he made a "follow me" sign, and the four of us began creeping quietly across the cavern, weaving in and out

among the bats. I kept picturing what might happen if they woke up and caught us. It was not a pretty picture.

Just as we reached the last row, the bat in front of Coop and me slowly opened its eyes and stared at us sleepily.

Coop quickly squeezed past him on the left and I squeezed past on the right. "Rock-a-bye baby," Coop whispered to him soothingly.

Then the four of us stepped rapidly through the wall.

But not to safety. We found ourselves standing on a narrow ledge next to a swirling black underground river. The roar of rushing water echoed off the walls.

"Hmmm," said Coop as he checked his direction finder.

"Let me guess," said Lootna. "We're going to have to cross the river, right?"

"Yep," said Coop. "And we'd better hurry. Batso's probably hot on our heels."

The river was too wide to jump at that point. And besides, there was no ledge on the other side—just the tunnel wall dropping straight down into the dark water. So we jogged along the ledge looking for a place to cross.

As we rounded a bend, we spotted two large rocks in the middle of the river. Coop didn't even break his stride. He just trotted along the ledge and made three running leaps—first to one rock, then to the other, then right through the far wall. He disappeared.

Finny, Lootna, and I followed after him.

CHAPTER  9

OOPS. NOT GOOD.

We had leaped right into a large cavern with about fifty Demon Bats. They were busy tossing each other over their shoulders and slamming each other down on floor mats. Shouts, grunts, and heavy thuds echoed off the stone walls.

We were in the middle of a hand-to-hand-combat class!

We skidded to a stop in front of a short, tough-looking bat with a whistle around his neck.

He scowled at us. Then he gave a loud blast on his whistle. All the other bats rushed over and crowded around us, looking fierce.

The one with the whistle poked Coop in the chest with his claw. "Just what do you think you're doing in my gym, buddy?" he growled. "You got business here, or what?"

"Why, of *course* we've got business here," said Coop. "We're, uh . . . let's see . . . we're working for General Batso. Aren't we, Jason?"

"You bet," I said. "General Batso hired us to, uh, teach you guys a new combat move."

I paused. I didn't know any combat moves, so I made one up. "It's called the Black Death Kick-Punch," I said.

The instructor bat snorted. "Never heard of it. And I don't need any wise guys to teach me anything. Here, watch this."

He picked up a rock the size of a football from the floor. He tossed it in the air. Then he leaped up and hacked the rock in two with his bare claw.

I heard Finny gulp. I think I gulped, too.

Coop yawned. "Not bad," he told the instructor bat. "I used to smash rocks that way myself—when I was a beginner. But then I learned the good old Black Death Kick-Punch. It's a high-speed, double-reverse, flying-corkscrew kick-punch. It's deadly. You should never leave home without it."

Coop cracked his knuckles.

"Oh, brother," muttered Lootna under her breath. "Mr. Karate Kid himself."

"I'll give you a little demonstration," Coop went on. He pointed to a nearby boulder that was about as high as his chest. "See that rock? Well, kiss it good-bye. It will soon be a pile of dust."

Coop gave a few practice chops in the air with his hand. *"Haiii-ya! Haiii-ya! Haiii-ya!"* he cried.

Then he dropped to the floor and did five quick push-ups. He leaped to his feet and did five quick jumping jacks. He smacked his fist into his hand twice. Then he flexed his muscles, smoothed down his hair, and touched his toes. "I'm ready," he said.

Lootna rolled her eyes.

Suddenly, from somewhere outside

the cavern we heard the sound of doors opening and slamming. Someone was making a search—for *us*.

"Actually," said Coop quickly, "a running start always helps. So I'll just jog down to the end of the cavern."

"This had better be good!" growled the instructor bat.

"Oh, I think you'll be impressed," said Coop. "Come on, team."

He started for the far wall at a fast clip. Lootna, Finny, and I ran along beside him.

We were almost there when the door flew open and General Batso and his men burst in. "Stop where you are!" yelled the general.

"Haiii-ya!" yelled Coop. And the four of us made flying leaps through the cavern wall.

But this time it wasn't so easy. This time I felt like I was moving slow-motion through molasses.

"I believe that's the last wall we can go through," said Finny after we were on the other side. "The effects of the walk-through-walls machine seem to be wearing off."

We looked around quickly. We were in a long, high tunnel.

At one end of it was a light.

Daylight!

CHAPTER **10**

WE RAN TOWARD
the opening for all we were worth.

Lootna raced out ahead and urged us on. "Come *on!*" she called.

"We're coming!" yelled Coop. "Believe me, we're coming!"

Finny was running along beside me, huffing and puffing. "Remind me to invent some flying shoes," he panted.

"Great idea," I panted back.

Suddenly we were there, at the end of the tunnel, looking out at the pale-green sky. We leaned out and peered down. Coop had led us back to the cliff, all right. We were in one of the eyeholes of the huge bat face. More than half a mile below us was the tossing yellow sea.

That's when we heard the nightmarish sound. We whirled around.

Flapping toward us at high speed was a screeching, screaming mob of Demon Bats. The tunnel was thick with them, some flying high, some low. The pink wings of General Batso were in the lead. Even at a distance I could see his red eyes blazing.

Coop pulled his remote-control device out of his pocket and tossed it to Lootna. "See if you can guide the spaceship down from the clouds," he told her. "Jason and I will try to keep Batso and his buddies busy."

Lootna caught the remote control with her tail. Then she turned toward the open sky and began rapidly pushing buttons with her paws.

I gulped. Keep the bats busy? How?

With a horrible scratching of toenails on stone, General Batso and his men landed in front of us. There must have been hundreds of them. Their fangs gleamed in the sunlight.

Batso gave an evil cackle and started toward us.

"Any ideas?" Coop whispered to me.

I thought fast. "Maybe," I whispered. Then I did the only thing I could think of. I put on my duck hat.

It was the Mr. Duckles the Duck hat that I'd bought from Arnold at his garage sale. I pulled it out of my pocket and slapped it on my head. The webbed feet flopped down over my ears. Then I whipped out my library card and flashed it at General Batso.

"You're under arrest," I told him.

Batso stopped short, looking startled.

"Allow me to introduce myself," I went on. "I am Inspector Duckles of the Galactic Police, Bat and Duck Division. Get your things together. We're taking you in."

General Batso eyed me suspiciously. Then he snorted. "Don't make me laugh. Why should I believe you're a cop?"

"Do you think I'd wear a dumb hat like this if I *wasn't*?" I asked him. "I wouldn't make any sudden moves if I were you, Batso." I jerked my thumb toward Coop. "This is my robot, Smasher. He's a high-tech killer-destroyer police robot, and

he's extremely dangerous."

Coop turned to me stiffly. He saluted. "Shall—I—take—these—twerps—apart —for—you—sir?" he asked in a slow, mechanical voice. "Shall—I— remove—their—heads—and—place— them—in—a—big—pile?"

"Easy, Smasher," I said. "Down, boy, down." I looked back at Batso. "Just keep your hands where I can see them, Batso. You're under arrest for planning to rob the Great Gold Vault on Vargas."

General Batso turned and glared at his men. "All right, who's been blabbing?"

"Don't blame them," I said with a steely smile. "We have our ways of finding things out. We know everything there is to know about you, fella."

"Oh, yeah?" growled Batso. "Well, you

don't scare me. In case you haven't noticed, there are four hundred of us and only four of you. What's to keep us from just throwing you off the cliff, mister bigshot detective?"

I narrowed my eyes. "My police robot, here, is worth four *thousand* of you," I warned him. "Touch one hair on this hat and Smasher will come down on you like a ton of bricks, mister."

"Time—to—smash?" asked Coop eagerly. "Time—to—crunch? Time—to—bash—this—big-mouthed—bozo—but—good?" He took a jerky step forward with his arms stretched out toward Batso. He flexed his fingers.

"No, Smasher!" I said. "Bad! Bad robot! You will bash that bozo when I give the command, and *only* when I give the command!"

"Ulp . . ." gulped General Batso. He took a little step backward.

"NOW!" cried Lootna.

I spun around. The spaceship was swooping toward us with the bubble top already open. As it slid past the entrance to the tunnel, it suddenly slowed almost to a stop.

Coop and I ran and jumped. Lootna was already inside. Finny dived after us.

We landed in a jumble. But in a split second Coop's hands were on the controls. The bubble top snapped shut, and the spaceship shot forward, swerving up and away from the cliff.

I looked back. A black cloud of bats was pouring out of the eyehole after us.

But a few moments later we were already going six hundred miles an hour. And far, far behind us, the Demon Bats of Bluggax looked like a harmless flock of small black birds.

CHAPTER 11

ON OUR WAY BACK to Earth we dropped Finny off at his laboratory. It was inside one of the six tiny moons that orbit the planet Mana-mana-ta.

Finny showed us around. His lab was enormous, and full of the strangest machines and tools and gizmos and whatzits I'd ever seen.

At the end of the tour Finny jumped up on a workbench and looked like he was going to make a speech. He was.

"My friends," he said with emotion, "I

cannot thank you enough. I asked you to rescue me, and rescue me you did. Therefore, as a token of my appreciation, I would like to present you with a small gift."

"No token necessary," said Coop. "What's a little rescue among friends?"

"No, no, I insist," said Finny. "And I have just the thing right here. It's one of my latest inventions, and I'm rather proud of it."

Lootna rolled her eyes. "Just leave me out of this," she said. "Leave me *way* out."

Finny jumped down and held out a thin golden rod with a jet-black tip. "I call it my Anti-Grav," he said.

"Sounds interesting," said Coop. "What's it do?"

"It makes things easy to lift," explained Finny. "Suppose you want to move a big, heavy table. All you do is touch the rod to the table, press this button, and presto! The table floats right off the ground. Then you push it wherever you want it to be, press another button, and it becomes heavy again. It's as simple as that."

"Wow," I said. "Will it work on anything?"

"Absolutely," said Finny. "Refrigerators, spaceships, robots, anything. Come to think of it, it would probably work on *living* things as well. Take Lootna, for instance."

Before Lootna could jump out of the way, Finny reached out, touched her with the tip of the Anti-Grav, and pressed the button. There was a humming sound and

then a crackling sound. And then a loud
pop!

And Lootna floated slowly into the air.

"What!" she sputtered. "What!"

"You see?" said Finny with delight.
"Light as a feather."

"You . . . you . . ." said Lootna as she
drifted higher and higher.

"Just like a balloon, isn't she?" said
Finny.

Lootna bounced lightly against the
ceiling. "Finny Ikkit, you pinhead! You
get me down from here!"

"Certainly," said Finny cheerfully. "No
problem at all. Can do and will do."

He fiddled with the Anti-Grav. Then he
gave it a shake. A wisp of black smoke
drifted out of the tip.

"We have a bit of a problem," Finny

called up to Lootna. "The Anti-Grav seems to be on the blink. I'm afraid you overloaded it and melted the circuits. But don't worry, Lootna. Don't blame yourself. It could happen to anyone. It's not your fault."

Lootna was bobbing sideways across the ceiling now. *"Fault?"* she sputtered, outraged. *"Fault?"*

"Perhaps you can bob over this way a bit," suggested Finny. "Then maybe I can stand on this chair and grab your tail."

"Perhaps you can stick your neck up here," said Lootna through clenched teeth. "Then maybe I can grab it and wring it for you!"

"She'll be all right," Finny said to Coop. "I can build another Anti-Grav within a week or two."

"A week!" shrieked Lootna. "Or *two*!"

"In the meantime," Finny told Coop, "you can go ahead and take her home with you. She'll be fine. But whenever you take her outside, you might want to tie a long string to her leg. Otherwise, there's no telling how high she might float."

"That does it!" yelled Lootna. "Let me at him! Hold him up here so I can get at him. I'll bust him in the nose! I'll tie his ears in a knot! I'll . . . I'll . . ."